The Little Red Hen

ADAPTED BY
Teresa Mlawer

ILLUSTRATED BY
Olga Cuéllar

Adirondack
Books

Once upon a time, there was a Little Red Hen who lived in a cottage with her five baby chicks. The cottage was near an old farm surrounded by trees and fields of golden wheat.

The Little Red Hen worked very hard. She kept her house very clean, and she always made sure her baby chicks had enough to eat.

On the farm lived a pig, a lamb, and a cat. Unlike the Little Red Hen, however, they were all very lazy.

They liked having a clean house and food on the table, but they never wanted to do any work.

One day, the Little Red Hen was sweeping her yard when she found some wheat kernels.

She immediately thought of planting them. She carefully put the kernels in her apron pocket and finished sweeping the yard.

Early the next morning, the Little Red Hen set out to plant
the wheat kernels. On her way, she passed by the farm and saw
her friends resting under a tree. She called to them and asked:

"Who will help me plant these wheat kernels?"

"Not I," said the pig.

"Not I," said the lamb.

"Not I," said the cat.

"Then I'll do it myself," said the Little Red Hen. And she did.

The Little Red Hen, along with her baby chicks, went to a nearby garden and began digging up the soil to plant the seeds.

Once the seeds were planted, she watered them.

"If we water the seeds, the wheat will grow, and we will have plenty to eat," said the Little Red Hen to her chicks.

Every day, the Little Red Hen went to the garden to water the seeds. Soon the wheat began to grow, and eventually it was time to harvest it. The Little Red Hen then asked her friends for help.

"Who will help me harvest the wheat?" she asked.

"Not I," said the pig.

"Not I," said the lamb.

"Not I," said the cat.

"Then I'll do it myself," said the Little Red Hen.

And she did.

The Little Red Hen filled her red wagon with the wheat, and on her way home she ran into her friends.

"Who will help me take the wheat to the mill?" she asked.

"Not I," said the pig.

"Not I," said the lamb.

"Not I," said the cat.

"Then I'll do it myself," said the Little Red Hen. And she did.

She went to the mill, along with her baby chicks, and she ground the wheat into flour.

When the Little Red Hen got home, she thought about what she would make with such fine flour. She decided to bake a nice loaf of bread for herself and her baby chicks. When the bread was ready, they would eat it with homemade strawberry jam.

Her friends followed her home from the mill. They were so curious that they came close and looked into her window.

When the Little Red Hen saw them, she asked, "Who will help me make this flour into dough for the bread?"

"Not I," said the pig.

"Not I," said the lamb.

"Not I," said the cat.

"Then I'll do it myself," said the Little Red Hen.
And she did.

She mixed the flour with other ingredients to make dough
for a nice loaf of bread.

Soon the house was filled with the delicious aroma
of freshly baked bread. Drawn in by the smell, the three
friends knocked on the window.

The Little Red Hen opened the window and asked,
"Who will help me eat this freshly baked loaf of bread?"

"I will," said the pig.

"I will," said the lamb.

"I will," said the cat.

"Oh no, you won't," said the Little Red Hen. You didn't help me plant the kernels, water the seeds, harvest the wheat, or mill it. You didn't help me make the dough or bake the bread.

Therefore, only my baby chicks and I will eat this delicious loaf of bread."

Soon after that, the Little Red Hen found some corn kernels in her yard. But this time, all her friends from the farm helped her plant the kernels, water the seeds, harvest the corn, and make delicious cornbread.

Once it was done, they celebrated together and ate the cornbread with some scrumptious hot chocolate.

What lesson have we learned from this story?

It's important to help others if you want to share in the rewards of hard work.

FOR INFORMATION, PLEASE CONTACT ADIRONDACK BOOKS, P.O. BOX 266, CANANDAIGUA, NEW YORK, 14424

ISBN 978-0-9864313-6-4   10 9 8 7 6 5 4 3 2 1   PRINTED IN CHINA